DISNEY fairies

TinkerBell

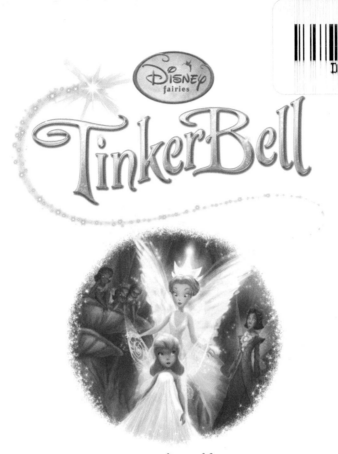

Adapted by
Andrea Posner-Sanchez

Illustrated by
Jeff Clark, Adrienne Brown, Charles Pickens,
and the Disney Storybook Artists

 A GOLDEN BOOK · NEW YORK

Copyright © 2011 Disney Enterprises, Inc. All rights reserved. Published in the United States by Golden Books, an imprint of
Random House Children's Books, a division of Random House, Inc., 1745 Broadway, New York, NY 10019, and in Canada by
Random House of Canada Limited, Toronto, in conjunction with Disney Enterprises, Inc. Golden Books, A Golden Book,
A Little Golden Book, the G colophon, and the distinctive gold spine are registered trademarks of Random House, Inc.
www.randomhouse.com/kids
ISBN: 978-0-7364-2761-6
Printed in the United States of America
10 9 8

Not so long ago, a baby laughed her first laugh.
That laugh flew out the window and attached itself to
a dandelion wisp. The wisp floated all the way from the
human world to Pixie Hollow, home of the Never fairies.
Once there, the laugh turned into a brand-new fairy!

All Never Fairies have a special talent. It was time for the new fairy to discover hers.

A hammer started to glow. Then it flew right into her hands.

"Come forward, tinker fairies," Queen Clarion called, "and welcome the newest fairy of your talent guild—Tinker Bell!"

Two other tinker fairies, Clank and Bobble,
showed Tinker Bell her new home in Tinkers' Nook.
"You've arrived at a most wondrous time—the
changing of the seasons!" they exclaimed.

Tink couldn't wait to get started! She put on a leaf dress, tied her hair up in a ponytail, and went to the tinkers' workshop. There she met Fairy Mary, the head of the tinkers. Then it was off to make deliveries to the nature fairies.

Clank, Bobble, and Tink brought pussy-willow brushes for Rosetta, milkweed-pod satchels for Fawn, and rainbow tubes for Iridessa. Tinker Bell was amazed as Iridessa created a rainbow and then rolled it up inside a tube.

"I'm taking the rainbow to the mainland to change the seasons," the light fairy told Tink.

Tink really wanted to be a nature fairy so she could go to the mainland, too. She asked Silvermist to teach her how to be a water fairy. But Tink broke every dewdrop she touched.

Iridessa tried to show Tink how to give light to
fireflies. But instead of making the fireflies light up,
Tink started to glow instead!

The animal fairy Fawn gave Tink a lesson in teaching baby birds to fly. But Tink couldn't even convince her bird to come out of its egg!

Tinker Bell was upset. "At this rate, I should get to the mainland right about, oh, *never!*" she complained as she walked along the beach.

Then Tink noticed a porcelain box filled with gears and springs.

When Tink's friends found her,
she was busy putting all the pieces
together. They watched quietly as Tink
attached a ballerina to the lid of the box. Suddenly,
the ballerina turned and the box played music. Tink
was the best tinker fairy they had ever seen!
But Tink still wanted to be a nature fairy.

Vidia, a mean fast-flying fairy, told Tink to gather the Sprinting Thistles. That would prove to everyone that she could be a garden fairy.

So Tink built a corral and locked some of the giant
weeds inside it. But Vidia blew the corral gate open and
the Thistles ran away! They stampeded through town,
destroying everything in their path.

Queen Clarion rushed over to see what had happened. The springtime supplies were ruined. There was no way they could bring spring to the mainland on time.

"I'm sorry," Tinker Bell whispered sadly before flying away.

Tinker Bell thought about leaving Pixie Hollow forever. But then she remembered putting the music box back together with all those found objects. Maybe she could make some machines that could get the springtime supplies ready super-fast! Tink got right to work.

The next morning, there were springtime supplies
everywhere. Tink had done it! Spring would arrive!
Then Clank and Bobble showed up with the music box.
"I ran across this myself many seasons ago," Fairy Mary said.
"I didn't have a clue how to fix it. But you did, Tinker Bell."
Fairy Mary and Queen Clarion agreed that Tink should go
to the mainland to return the music box to its owner.

When Tink and the other fairies arrived in London, everything looked dull and gray. But as the nature fairies did their jobs, ice melted, flowers bloomed, birds chirped, and marvelous colors appeared! It was even more beautiful than Tink had imagined.

As Tink flew past a row of houses, the music box started to glow outside a bedroom window. Tink set the box on the windowsill, tapped on the glass, and hid. Soon a girl appeared, thrilled to find her long-lost music box.

Tink's work was done. She loved being a tinker fairy!